PUT YOUR WORRIES IN A BOX

Written by Pam Harrison

D1451725

This Book is Dedicated to
My Family

I am playing with my friends, soaking up the sun...

When all of a sudden, I realize
I am not having fun.

I feel a prickle on my skin, my face becomes hot, my stomach feels like it's tied in a knot.

And all I want is for these feelings to stop!

I tell my mom, I tell my dad, and I tell Grandma and Grandpa that I am sad. "What's wrong?" they say.

"I don't want to play, maybe we can come back another day?"

"Oh no, oh my," my parents sigh.

With a big deep breath, I quietly say, "the loud noises scare me away. The bugs in the grass, the cars racing by, and the dark, dark sky all ruin my day."

"Ok," my parents say, "then let's not stay."

When I am home, I sit on my bed, still thinking about the worries in my head.

My mom comes in, she sits on my bed, "look here," she says, and lays a box on the bed.

She leans in and says, "gather your worries, don't give them another thought, just push them front and center and dump them in this box!"

I close my eyes and do what she says.

Holding the box high, over my head,
I reach up and set it on the shelf
over my bed.

And then I feel my body turn warm with the thought that my worries will stay closed in that box.

Made in United States
North Haven, CT
25 October 2021